MY LiFe
as a
Supersized Superhero
... WITH SLOBBER

Books by Bill Myers

Series

SECRET AGENT DINGLEDORF
... and his trusty dog, SPLAT

The Case of the . . .

Giggling Geeks • Chewable Worms
• Flying Toenails • Drooling Dinosaurs •
Hiccupping Ears • Yodeling Turtles

The Incredible Worlds of Wally McDoogle

My Life As . . .

a Smashed Burrito with Extra Hot Sauce • Alien Monster Bait
• a Broken Bungee Cord • Crocodile Junk Food •
Dinosaur Dental Floss • a Torpedo Test Target
• a Human Hockey Puck • an Afterthought Astronaut •
Reindeer Road Kill • a Toasted Time Traveler
• Polluted Pond Scum • a Bigfoot Breath Mint •
a Blundering Ballerina • a Screaming Skydiver
• a Human Hairball • a Walrus Whoopee Cushion •
a Computer Cockroach (Mixed-Up Millennium Bug)
• a Beat-Up Basketball Backboard • a Cowboy Cowpie •
Invisible Intestines with Intense Indigestion
• a Skysurfing Skateboarder • a Tarantula Toe Tickler •
a Prickly Porcupine from Pluto • a Splatted-Flat Quarterback
• a Belching Baboon • a Stupendously Stomped Soccer Star •
a Haunted Hamburger, Hold the Pickles
• a Supersized Superhero . . . with Slobber •

THE IMAGER CHRONICLES

The Portal • The Experiment • The Whirlwind • The Tablet

Picture Book
Baseball for Breakfast

www.Billmyers.com

the incredible worlds of **Wally McDoogle**

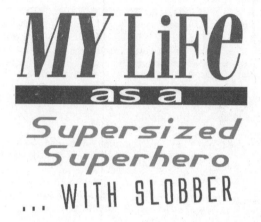

MY LiFe
as a
Supersized
Superhero
... WITH SLOBBER

BILL MYERS

THOMAS NELSON
Since 1798

NASHVILLE DALLAS MEXICO CITY RIO DE JANEIRO BEIJING

Published in Nashville, TN, by Thomas Nelson. Thomas Nelson is a
trademark of Thomas Nelson, Inc.

Thomas Nelson, Inc. titles may be purchased in bulk for educational,
business, fund-raising, or sales promotional use. For information,
please email SpecialMarkets@ThomasNelson.com.

Unless noted otherwise, all Scripture references are from the
International Children's Bible®, *New Century Version*®, © 1986, 1988,
1999 by Thomas Nelson, Inc. All rights reserved.

Library of Congress Cataloging-in-Publication Data

Myers, Bill, 1953–
   My life as a supersized superhero—with slobber / Bill Myers.
      p. cm.— (The incredible worlds of Wally McDoogle ; 28)
   Summary: Believing that God wants him to make the world a better
place, Wally is thrilled when Junior Whiz Kid outfits him with a
supersuit, but he soon realizes that everyday acts of kindness make
more of a difference than a superhero ever could.
   ISBN-13: 978-1-4003-0637-4 (pbk.)
   ISBN-10: 1-4003-0637-X
   [1. Heroes—Fiction. 2. Inventions—Fiction. 3. Christian Life—
Fiction. 4. Humorous stories.] I. Title.
   PZ7.M98234Mylem 2007
   [Fic]—dc22

                                          2007005540

Printed in the United States of America

07 08 09 10 11 RRD 9 8 7 6 5 4 3

For Janey and Louis DeMeo . . .
who know the real secret of serving the King.

Contents

"I tell you the truth. Anything you did for any of my people here, you also did for me."

—Matthew 25:40

Chapter 1

Just for Starters

I was having another one of my world-famous *day*mares.

It would have been nightmares, but I was sitting in Mr. Reptenson's science class . . . which meant I was required to catch up on my sleep. I don't want to say that it's a law or anything, but the U.S. Surgeon General had posted a sign on his door that read:

WARNING: *Listening to this teacher may cause great boredom, resulting in serious eye glazing, loss of consciousness, and little puddles of drool forming on your desk from sleeping with your mouth open.*

It's not that Reptile Man (that's what we call him for short) is boring. But if you ever want to chill down after an exciting day of watching snail races or the leaves changing color, his classroom is just the place.

So, there I was, conked out on my desk making my own little drool pool, when suddenly I heard tap-dancing.

I pried open my baby blues and saw an angel in a white tuxedo, top hat, and cane tap-dancing on Reptile Man's desk.

"Bartholomew!" I cried.

"Good afternoon, Wallace." He spoke in his usual thick English accent.

Of course, Mr. Reptenson didn't notice a thing. It's hard noticing things like tap-dancing angels when you're only wearing a scuba suit, passing out answers to all upcoming quizzes, and showing *Spider-Man XVII* on a giant-screen TV that you traded in your blackboard for.

(Oh, yeah, I was definitely dreaming.)

"So, how's the angel biz?" I asked.

"Smashing," he said, continuing his dance. "By the way, I loved your *My Life As Reindeer Road Kill* book."

"I mentioned you in it."

"My point exactly. Of course, it's not exactly the same as being in *the* Book with Gabriel and the other guys, but . . ."

"*The* Book?" I asked.

"The Bible, Wallace."

"Oh, yeah, *that* the Book."

"Not as many laughs as yours, but definitely worth the read."

I nodded. "Where did you learn to dance like that?"

"Oh, this?" He did a flurry of tapping. "I've been watching old Shirley Temple movies."

I glanced around the room and saw every kid in class was playing video games on monitors that were built into their desks. Not only that, but the cafeteria lady was going around serving pizza with a crust that was actually fit for human consumption.

Yes, I was definitely dreaming.

"Listen, Wallace, I have another invitation for you from God."

I suddenly got a little nervous. Remembering my numerous near-death experiences from the last one, I asked, "What is it this time?"

He opened his hand to reveal a glowing envelope. Instantly, it turned into a pigeon and flew across the room where it landed on my shoulder. Talk about cool. It was even cooler when it turned back into the invitation.

I took the invitation and read:

The Lord requests your help in making the world a better place to live.

"God wants me to help . . . Him?!" I asked in astonishment.

Bartholomew nodded.

"Wow! What an honor! Why me?"

"Rumor has it He likes the underdogs. And they don't come any more *under* than you."

I nodded. When he was right, he was right. "But how can I help make the world a better place to live?"

"He will show you when the time is right," Bartholomew said as he started to fade.

"Wait a minute, don't leave!" I jumped to my feet. "God wants me to help Him?"

"That's right."

"But . . . what about tools or weapons and stuff? What am I supposed to use?"

"Your tools will be provided. . . ."

"But . . . wait a minute! You gotta tell me more! I need more information!"

"Well, Wally, this is a pleasant surprise," Mr. Reptenson said.

I blinked. "Huh?"

Bartholomew was gone, and I was standing beside my desk with Mr. Reptenson talking to me: "I appreciate your wanting more information. Stay after class and I'll be happy to discuss, in greater detail, the unique and fascinating process of photosynthesis."

"Thanks . . . ," I squeaked as my face kinda turned beet red as my body kinda melted back into my seat.

That was the bad news. The good news was, Bartholomew had only been a dream. Or so I thought. . . .

* * * * *

If you've ever watched old westerns on TV and seen cattle stampedes, you know what our school hallway is like when the lunch bell rings.

My best friend Opera, aka the Human Eating Machine, and I had just joined the herd, trying not to get trampled, when a little voice beside me said:

"Mister McDoogle! *cough-sniff*, Mister McDoogle!"

I looked down to see little Willy Runeenoze beside me. He'd been sick for just under a gazillion years and had returned to school. The bad news was, he was so behind in his work that unless he got a tutor, they'd hold him back a year. The badder news was, Principal Yellinyerface thought I'd be the perfect tutor to help him catch up with his studies.

So, a day or so ago I had promised to help . . . just as soon as I found a free minute.

"Mister McDoogle? *sniff-cough*, Mister McDoogle."

"Willy," I said, "will you please stop calling me *Mister*."

"I'm sorry, *sneeze-wheeze*. How 'bout *Sir*? Is Sir McDoogle okay?"

It kinda had a catchy ring to it, so I nodded.

"Can I come over to your place for help on my homework tonight?"

"Not tonight," I said. "God needs me to save the world for Him."

"Oh, *wheeze-sneeze*. What about afterward? I can stay up till nine o'clock."

He looked up to me—so eager, so hopeful (so uninformed of my reputation as the Disaster Master). What could I do? Break the little guy's heart? No way. So, I did the next best thing. I lied. "Yeah, sure."

"All right!" He broke into a round of joyous hacking. "Because I really need—"

"Hey, Wally!"

Willy's hack attack was interrupted by Wall Street, my other best friend (even though she is a girl). "I just got a call from Junior Whiz Kid," she said as she joined us.

Just the sound of his name made me colder than an ice cube in a freezer in the middle of Antarctica . . . on a cloudy day.

"What's *he* want?" Opera asked, chomping away on his third bag of Chippy Chipper potato chips. (It was taking longer than normal to get to the cafeteria, so he'd broken into the emergency stash of chips taped to his belly under his shirt.)

"He's got a new invention he wants to try out on Wally."

I shivered. "Why me?"

"Because you've worked with him before. Once with that rocket-powered skateboard that nearly killed you, and once with that giant tarantula . . . that nearly killed you."

"They were both disasters," I argued.

Wall Street shrugged. "I guess he believes the third time's the charm."

"Or," Opera suggested, "three strikes and you're out."

(Opera doesn't always look at the bright side of things.)

"Relax," Wall Street said. "I've taken out a good insurance policy on you."

"Meaning?"

"Meaning if you die, I get a bazillion bucks."

"WHAT?!" I didn't mean to yell, but I always get a little touchy when best friends plan my death.

"No, no," she said. "This time it's cool. Junior

says he's got all sorts of superhero weapons he wants to hook you up to."

"Superhero . . . *weapons*?"

"Yeah, to fight against the forces of evil and help make the world a better place."

The phrase sounded more than a little familiar. "He said *that*?"

"Yeah, along with the fact that it's been a while since any of his inventions backfired, and he needs a few laughs."

I looked at her, and she shrugged.

It was obvious Wall Street was using me . . . again. But it was equally obvious that Junior could provide exactly what Bartholomew had promised . . . a way to make the world a better place. Of course, I was more nervous than a worm in the middle of a fishing-hook convention. But, let's face it, there are worse things that could happen than being hurt as a superhero.

(At the moment none come to mind, so I'll have to get back to you on that.)

The point is, Wall Street might be right— maybe the third time really is the charm.

Then again, there was Opera's comment about baseball and three strikes.

But since I'm allergic to sports (I break out in a bad case of broken bones every time I get near them), I bought what Wall Street was selling instead.

Unfortunately, I was about to find out there were no refunds and all sales were final.

Chapter 2

An Old Fiend

After winding through creepy dark streets that gave me the chills, and chilly dark alleys that gave me the creeps, we finally arrived at Junior Whiz Kid's laboratory.

"Go ahead and knock," Wall Street said.

I nodded and

knock-knock-knocked

on the door—all the time praying my little heart out. There was no answer, so once again I

knock-knock-knocked.

"Okay, Wally, that's enough knocking."

I nodded and

knock-knock-knocked

some more.

"Wally, enough already."

I nodded in full agreement. But the *knock*ing had nothing to do with the door or my knuckles. Instead, it had everything to do with fear and my

knock-knock-knocking

knees.

The good news was, it finally stopped.

The bad news was, it was replaced by a slightly louder and more obnoxious

ZZZZZZZZZAAPPPP
K-BLEWIE!

If you guessed that was the sound of a laser beam blowing up the door, you'd have guessed right. And if you guessed that standing on the other side of the door was seven-year-old Junior Whiz Kid, then maybe you should stop reading this book and start writing your own.

"A pleasant afternoon to you, Wally." Although Junior was only seven, he had the vocabulary of a seventy-year-old. On his head was a football helmet with a miniature camera lens attached to the top. But instead of shooting pictures, the lens was shooting

ZZZZZZZZZAAPPP ZZZZZZZZZAAPPP ZZZZZZZZZAAPPP
K-BLEWIE

beams.

(If you guessed that one, you definitely need to be a writer . . . or see a good brain doctor.)

"Dreadfully sorry about that," Junior apologized while accidentally

ZZZZZZZZZAAPPPPPing
and K-BLEWIEing

up the next-door neighbor's wall. No problem, except it belonged to some granny's bathroom . . . which wouldn't have been so bad except Granny was in the middle of her daily

"EEEEEK!"

shower.

At last he found the off switch. He hit it five or six times, but with no result. Luckily, he had a nearby baseball bat, which he

K-thud, K-thud, K-thudded

a few more times, giving himself a major headache, but finally shutting the thing down.

Fortunately, he didn't knock himself out.

Unfortunately, he reached out to shake my hand.

Don't get me wrong, I like being as friendly as the next guy. But when the hand is a mechanical arm that

K-ZIIIING!

shoots out at a thousand miles an hour, forcing you to

"AUGH!"

duck as it keeps going another mile or two, stopping at nothing, including more bathroom walls . . . with more folks taking showers (not to mention other bathroom things) . . . well, you can see why it might make a cowardly person like myself just a bit more, oh, I don't know . . . cowardly.

"Please," Junior said, pulling the mechanical arm back in, "do come in."

I tried to move, but my body had this thing about wanting to live.

Unfortunately, Wall Street had this thing about wanting to make a gazillion dollars. "It's good to see you again," she said as she stepped inside.

Junior turned to me. "Please, Wally, join us."

I didn't know which was worse—admitting I was scared to death of some seven-year-old kid, or having my heart stop 'cause I was scared to death of some seven-year-old kid. Either way, my feet finally decided to obey—which was good for my ego, but not so good for my health.

Wall Street motioned to the smoking door, the blown-out walls, and all the screaming wet and naked people. "What was that about?"

"Just my latest invention," Junior explained.

Wall Street nodded. "Looks like you still have a few bugs to work out."

"Yes and no."

"What do you mean?"

"Yes, there are a few bugs to work out; but no, because as soon as I surgically implant them into Wally's body, they will work perfectly."

"What?!" I screamed sorta hysterically.

"Relax." Junior laughed sorta creepily.

Unfortunately, the laugh loosened his helmet's on/off switch, which sorta caused a few more

ZZZZZZZZZAAPPPPs
K-BLEWIEs,

which sorta ruined the privacy of a few more neighbors, which sorta caused Junior to grab the bat and do a few more

K-thud, K-thud, K-thuddings

until everything shut down . . . including my ability to stand.

It's not that my emotions had overloaded and I passed out or anything. But with all the fear and terror I was feeling, I really saw no need to stick around and stay conscious.

* * * * *

The nice thing about having an imagination is that there's always something for you to do . . . even when you're knocked out. So, not liking to waste time, I immediately went to work on one of my superhero stories. . . .

It is a normally non-unnormal morning in the unnormally normal home of the unnormally non-unnormal Normal Dude.

TRANSLATION: Things are pretty normal.

Normal Dude hits his snooze alarm for the fifth time as Sister 1 screams at Sister 2 for hogging the bathroom,

while Sister 3 screams at Sister 1 for
re-stealing her sweater, which Sister
2 stole in the first place, which
explains why one of them (by now I've
lost track) is breaking into tears and
sobbing, "I think I'm getting a pimple
on my nose!"

(If you're trying to make sense out
of this, you obviously don't have sisters. If you do have sisters, then you
know this is perfectly...normal.)

Suddenly, someone is

*knock-knock-knock*ing

at the front door.

"I'll get it!" Sister 1, 2, or 3
shrieks. (They all sound the same when
they're shrieking, which is also pretty
normal.)

What is NOT normal is...

fisssowitzzzz...

suddenly, Normal Dude is no longer
playing tag with his snooze alarm.
Instead, he is at the table with the
rest of the family eating breakfast.

Of course, the girls do their normal screaming and panic-attack stuff while Normal Dude, with a mouthful of blueberry muffin, simply asks, "Muff juss mapppened?"

"I don't know," Sis 1 cries. "I was at the front door and found this remote control that someone left. It only has one button labeled fast forward, so I just pressed it like this

fisssowitzzzz...

and suddenly the entire family is heading back up the stairs to get ready for school."

"Cool!" Sis 2 shouts.

"But I missed eating!" Sis 3 cries.

"With your weight, you could stand missing a few meals," Sis 1 snickers.

"Mom!"

"Better fat than looking like Rudolph the Red-Nosed Reindeer," Sis 2 says, pointing at Sis 1's pimple.

"MOM!!"

Soon everyone is crying and doing their drama-queen routine until Mom grabs the remote, presses it, and

fisssowitzzzz...

everyone is dressed and heading out
the front door.

Mom beams at the remote and says,
"Well, now I know what I want for
Christmas! Talk about cool!"

What is not cool is that everyone
else in the neighborhood also has a
remote, which explains why

fisssowitzzzz...

everybody was suddenly sitting in
class. (Apparently, someone didn't like
walking to school.)

fisssowitzzzz...

Well, we *were* sitting in class. Now
we're at the lunch table. But apparently, lunch isn't someone's favorite
pastime, either, so

fisssowitzzzz...

now we're heading home,

fisssowitzzzz...

make that watching TV,

fisssowitzzzz...

lying in bed,

fisssowitzzzz...

eating breakfast,

fisssowitzzzz...

eating lunch.

Finally, Normal Dude's cell phone rings. Faster than you can say, "I thought we'd never get done reading those stupid *fisssowitzzzz* sound effects, and is *fisssowitzzzz* really a sound?" our abnormally nice and never-negative Normal Dude flips open his phone and answers with his favorite superhero slogan:

"Think dramatic is icky?
Try Normal and yell, 'Yippee!'"
(Hey, he's a superhero, not a poet.)

"Normal Dude!"

Our hero immediately recognizes the voice. "Mister President, is that you? What's going on?"

The President answers, "The notoriously not-so-nice guy Fast Forward Fiend has just escaped from the prison for the criminally lame."

"You don't mean..."

"Yes, he is flooding the country with Fast Forward Fiend remotes! Soon people will no longer have to wait for anything!"

"Why is that a problem?"

"Because——"

fisssowitzzzz...

Suddenly, Normal Dude is off the phone and back in bed——

fisssowitzzzz...

make that school——

fisssowitzzzz...

the weekend...*fisssowitzzzz*...spring

break...*fisssowitzzzz*...summer vaca...
fisssowitzzzz...

Well, you get the picture. If our
hero is going to save the day...*fisssowitzzzz*—er, night...*fisssowitzzzz*...er,
year, he must act now, while there are
still a few years left...*fisssowitzzzz*...
make that a few decades left...*fisssowitzzzz*...

Forget it. I'll catch you in the next
superhero section.

fisssowitzzzz...

Chapter 3

Extreme Makeover

When I finally regained consciousness, I raised my head. "What . . . what happened?" I asked. Only then did I notice I was lying on an operating table. (Not a good sign.)

"I can't believe it," Wall Street said. "You're still alive!" (Another not-good sign.)

"How do you feel?" Junior Whiz Kid asked from the other side of the table. "Can you sit up?"

"I think so." I rose and with his help threw my legs over the side of the table. They made a strange

K-Clank
K-Creak
K-Groaning

sound. (I'm guessing another not-so-good sign.)

"You just need a little oil," Junior said.

I frowned and looked down at my body. Well, what used to be my body. Now it looked a lot like a giant can of green beans . . . with me as the beans! Of course, this led to my ever-popular and patent-pending . . .

"AUGH!!"

"Relax," Wall Street said.

I wanted to obey but wasn't sure how a can of green beans relaxes!

"What did you do to my body?" I yelled.

"Oh, it's still in there . . . somewhere."

"Somewhere?! Where's the *there* in the some-where?"

"The *there* is in there somewhere."

"In there somewhere is where the *there* is?"

Junior shrugged. "Somewhere."

We were getting nowhere fast (which was worse than somewhere slow) until Wall Street finally stepped in. "The good news is, Junior didn't surgically implant the superhero tools into your body after all."

I nodded. "And the bad news?"

"He surgically implanted your body into the superhero tools."

"*HE WHAT?!*"

"Don't worry," Junior said. "We can cut you out of there anytime you want."

"Anytime like this time?!"

"This time could be anytime, though in time the right anytime might—"

"Stop it!" I shouted. "We've already done that bit!" With effort I slid off the table and

K-Clank, K-Creak, K-Groan

fell flat on my

K-Rash

you guessed it . . . can.

I rolled onto my back and groaned, "How can I save the world dressed up like some *Wizard of Oz* character?"

"Check out your right hand," Junior said.

I looked down at my hand. Well, what used to be my hand. Now it was . . .

"A GIANT DRILL BIT!" I screamed.

"I decided not to give you a mechanical arm, but a giant drill," he said proudly.

"That's terrible!" I shouted.

"Why's that?"

"Why's that? *Why's that?!*" It took me a moment before I finally came up with an answer. "How will I brush my teeth?" (Okay, it wasn't such a great answer, but at least it was a start.)

"Wally . . ."

"Or floss!" I cried. "You know how important flossing is?" (Now I was on a roll.)

"Wally!"

"And my penmanship! This will definitely not improve my penmanship!"

"WALLY!"

I stopped and looked at Wall Street.

"Try moving your hand," she said.

"I don't have a hand!"

"It's under your suit. Just try moving it."

"Like this?" I asked.

Suddenly, the drill bit started to

RRRRRR . . .

turn. I moved my hand some more, and it

RRRRRRed

some more.

That was kinda cool, though I wasn't exactly sure what it would be good for.

"Now rise," Junior said, "and allow me to display to you other features of your supersuit—such as the LASER EYE BLASTER."

I put my hands on the floor to get up. At least that's what I wanted to do. Unfortunately, when I used my right hand it

RRRRRRRRed

even more. No problem, except for the part of drilling into Junior's floor. I pushed even harder trying to get up, which caused even more

RRRRRRRRRRRing.

"Wally, stop!"

Before I could obey, the drill got stuck and quit spinning. That was the good news. But, as we all know, there's only one thing that follows good news. . . .

Since the drill was stuck but the motor was still turning, there was only one thing left to spin. And that one thing could only be

> *RRRRRR* . . .
> "Whoa!"
> *RRRRRR* . . .
> "Whaaa!"
> *RRRRRR* . . .
> "Wheee!"

me.

"Stop it!" Junior cried. "Stop it at once!"

But, of course, I didn't know how to stop it, which would explain Junior jumping on my back to help, which only led to both of us

"Whoa!"ing,
"Whaaa!"ing,
and "Wheee!"ing

along with the drill participating in its ever-popular

*RRRRRRRRRRRRRRRRR*ing.

"HOW DO YOU TURN IT OFF?" I shouted.

"DISCONNECT THE POWER?" Wall Street yelled.

"YOU CANNOT!" Junior explained. "YOU MUST WAIT FOR THE BATTERY TO DIE."

"WHEN WILL THAT BE?" I shouted.

"TWO OR THREE HOURS!"

Since time is money (and money is all Wall Street has time for), she leaped in. Using some of her strength (which is a lot more than all of mine), she was able to pull the drill out of the wood.

Of course, the drill was still spinning—but we weren't. Something we were all grateful for.

"Thank you so very much," Junior said.

"No problem," Wall Street answered.

Unfortunately, the fun and games weren't exactly over. Since I wasn't exactly the happiest of campers (or human drills), I scrunched my eyebrows into a frown.

"No, Wally," Junior shouted. "Do not frown!"

"What?"

"Your frown muscles are attached to the LASER EYE BLASTER!"

I didn't understand, which made me frown harder. "*What?*"

"NO!"

Suddenly, a red glass dropped in front of my eye, and a laser beam shot

ZZZZZZZZZAAPPPP
K-BLEWIE

out of it.

Yes sir, it was just like old times. And remember that little old lady we caught taking a shower in her bathroom? Well, now we were suddenly watching her

"EEEEEK!"

dressing in her bedroom.

"Sorry!" I shouted, frowning harder.

"Wally, no—"

ZZZZZZZZZAAPPPP
K-BLEWIE!

There went her bed in a puff of smoke.
"Sorry . . ."

ZZZZZZZZZAAPPPP
K-BLEWIE!

And say good-bye to her closet.
Then last, but not least, there went

ZZZZZZZZZAAPPPP

her dresser.

But, strangely enough, there was no explo-
sion. The reason was simple. My little laser beam
didn't hit the dresser, but the dresser mirror. So,
instead of blowing it up, the laser reflected right
back at

K-BLEWIE

me. Which explains why I once again decided to
drop by and visit the Land of Unconsciousness.

* * * * *

I woke up inside a racing van that was throwing my tin-can body from one side

roll-roll-roll
K-CLANK!

to the

roll-roll-roll
K-LUNK!

other. That was the good news.

I looked at the driver's seat and saw Junior below the wheel. (He should have been *behind* the wheel, but, like I said, he is only seven.)

"What's going on?" I shouted. "Where are we going?"

"The police radio said there's a bank robbery in progress," Wall Street yelled from the passenger side. "And you're going to stop it."

(Well, now we know the bad news.)

"There they are!" she shouted. "Stop the car!"

Junior hit the brakes while I, of course,

roll-roll-roll
K-HIT!

the windshield.

Then, being the kind, sensitive friend Wall Street is, she shouted, "Stop clowning around, Wally! It's time to be a superhero!"

To help make her point, she opened the door and sorta kicked me out.

To prove I got her point, I sort of

roll-roll-rolled

across the street until I smashed into somebody's leg. Somebody's leg attached to somebody's body that was attached to somebody's face in a ski mask.

But it wasn't the ski mask that worried me. Nor the fact that I had managed to scratch and dent my brand-new superhero body. It was what Mr. Ski Mask held in his hand that made me nervous. Not the hand with the big sack of money—but the other hand.

The one with the big gun . . . the big gun that was pointed down at me.

"Hi, there," I kinda mumbled.

"Grrr," he kinda growled.

Ever have one of those days?

(Unfortunately, I seem to have one of those lives.)

Chapter 4

A Sticky Stickup

"Get up," Mr. Ski Mask ordered.

Remembering what I did to Junior's lab floor, I tried to explain. "I really don't think you want me to."

"NOW!"

Having been taught to honor my elders (especially the ones with ski masks and guns), I reluctantly obeyed. I put my hands on the ground and began to push up, which immediately started my drill

RRRRRR . . .

spinning.

Unfortunately, drilling into an asphalt road is a little harder than a wooden floor.

Actually, it wasn't the drilling that was the problem.

It was the getting stuck.

Once again the drill could no longer turn, which, of course, left yours truly to do all the

"Whoaaa! Whaaaaa! Wheeeee!"

work.

On the McDoogle Scale of Fun, I'd give it about a .000½—rating it just below getting dumped along with a truckload of spinach into a giant blender and being squished into a tube of Spinach Toothpaste. (Hey, with me, it could happen.)

Still, all that turning did come in handy for spinning around and knocking down Mr. Ski Mask again and again . . . and again some more.

We could have drilled like this forever (or at least until I struck oil), but his partner pulled up in a getaway car and shouted, "Get in!"

Mr. Ski Mask rolled out of my way, got up, and leaped inside the car.

I wanted to join them, but I only had a few more thousand miles to go before I hit China, which I hear is really pretty this time of year.

The getaway car squealed off, and the cops began pursuit.

Meanwhile, Wall Street, always full of helpful ideas, shouted out her best advice ever: "Wally, do something!"

I nodded, frowning to think.

"NO!" Junior cried. "DO NOT FROWN! DO NOT—"

ZZZZZZZZZAAPPPP
K-BLEWIE!

There went the bank building, then

ZZZZZZZZZAAPPPP
K-BLEWIE

the Quickie Mart across the street, then

ZZZZZZZZZZAAPPPP
K-BLEWIE

a nearby car.

Yes sir, I was blowing up more things than a terrorist on steroids. Next up was a gas station. Knowing that couldn't be good, I manipulated my magnificent McDoogle Mind.

TRANSLATION: I thought for a change.

I kinda glanced down at the asphalt that my drill was stuck in . . . which kinda

ZZZZZZZZZAAPPPP
K-BLEWIEd

it up . . . which kinda freed my hand . . . which kinda threw me staggering backward.

Ah, free at last!

(If you buy that, then you obviously haven't read enough of these stories.)

I kept staggering backward until I hit the propane tank at the back of the gas station. The good news was, I didn't frown at it. The bad news was, my hand hit it, and I sorta

RRRRRRed

a little hole into it.

No biggie,

> . . . except for the *hisssss* of propane shooting through it,
> . . . and the sparks flying from my metal drill bit,
> . . . and the fact that sparks and propane don't play nicely together.

To make a long story short (but just as painful), the *hissss*ing propane caught fire and created the first rocket-powered propane tank. That's right, it broke from its stand and shot up faster than the hand of a first grader in class who has to use the bathroom.

It felt great knowing I'd make the history books as the inventor of the very first rocket-powered propane tank. It did *not* feel great knowing those same books would include me as its first passenger.

But since my hand was stuck in the tank, I didn't have a lot of choices but to practice my tried-and-true

"AUGHHHHH!"

while shooting above the highway at just under the speed of light.

Now, I don't want to complain, but the in-flight service was terrible—no movie, no soft drinks, not even those miniature peanut bags holding a grand total of 3½ peanuts. Still, the view was pretty good, and I did like the interactive video game. You know, the one where you frown down at the cars on the road below with your LASER EYE BLASTER, and you kinda *K-BLEWIE* them up?

Actually, that wasn't my intention. I was more than happy to see the police cars closing in on the bad guys. I would have been happier than happy if each time I saw one of those police cars, I hadn't frowned and accidentally *K-BLEWIE*d them up.

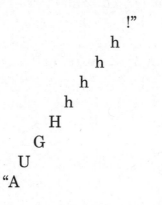

the officers screamed as they shot into the air.
  "Sorry!" I shouted as they sailed past.

the officers screamed as they shot into the air.

they yelled as they arced over my head and dropped back

K-Rash!

down.

The bad guy's car raced just ahead. I was closing in fast when suddenly, *K-sputter, K-sputter, K-sputter,* my trusty propane tank ran out of fuel. With no warning, not even a FASTEN YOUR SEAT BELT. WE'RE ALL GOING TO DIE sign, I dropped out of the sky and directly onto

K-Lunk

you guessed it, the car.

The good news was, the impact loosened my drill from the propane tank. The bad news was, when I tried to get up, I immediately shoved the bit into the car's roof. (Don't you just hate it when that happens?)

Of course, the bad dudes looked up at me and did the usual bad-dude shouting:

"Hey, you (*insert bad-dude language here*), what (*insert more bad-dude language here*) do you think you're doing?" (Their moms obviously let them watch way too many R-rated movies.)

I wanted to explain that these types of McDoogle Mishaps were only natural (like earthquakes and hurricanes) and that if they would be patient, I'd either pass out or die. But, since the drill was still spinning, I could only answer with my usual, "Whoa!"ing, "Whaaa!"ing, and "Wheee!"ing.

Still, all good things must come to an end.

In my case, it was the end of the road. It turned left, but the bad-guy driver was so busy shouting bad-guy things up at me that he didn't see and just kept on driving straight— which can really get interesting, especially when straight involves shooting off a 3,000-foot cliff.

Once again, I was flying high. This time attached to a car. And since my drill was still stuck in the top of the car's roof and the car was no longer on the ground, the vehicle started spinning instead of me!

What a nice change of pace.

And, since the bad guys had done more bad-guy things, like not fastening their seat belts, they were flung out their doors screaming more bad-guy stuff and throwing in a few

"AUGH!"s

for the kiddies in the audience.

The good news was, we all landed in the tops of some

Crack! Thud! "Ooaf!"

trees.

The better news was, the battery in my drill
had finally started to die.

And the best news?

I really wasn't in that bad of shape.

TRANSLATION: I only needed one emergency trip to the hospital and seven major
surgeries.

Unfortunately, even greater news was on the
way.

* * * * *

"Mister McDoogle, look this way!"

I sorta turned my head on the hospital pil-
low and was sorta

K-FLASH, K-FLASH, K-FLASH

blinded by a thousand cameras going off. Then
there were the thousand and one TV crews with
their thousand and one reporters all talking at
once:

"How does it feel to be a hero?"

"What's it like to be a hotshot!"
"Where do you get such incredible courage?"

I squinted into the lights and frowned. (Luckily, I didn't blow anybody up.) By the looks of things, the doctors had removed any trace of my LASER EYE BLASTER. They'd also replaced my superhero suit of metal with a suit of plaster. (They do that sort of thing when you break every bone in your body.)

Another reporter asked, "Were all those death-defying stunts scary?"

I shook my head. "I'm used to it. Having a black belt in self-destruction makes even getting out of bed a death-defying stunt, so—"

Wall Street stepped in. "What my client means to say is, this is only the beginning. As soon as he recovers, he'll be performing death-defying stunts every day." She turned to me. "Isn't that right, Wonder Wimp?"

I looked at her and blinked. "*Wonder what?*"

The reporters continued pressing in until she held out her hands. "Please, please, no more questions for now. Wonder Wimp needs his rest."

I looked at her in surprise. Could it be? For the first time in history, was Wall Street more worried about my welfare than making money?

"You'll have plenty of time to talk to him

once we've sold all the locks of his hair and auctioned off his remaining blood samples to the highest bidder."

Good ol' Wall Street. Some things never change.

Reluctantly, everyone shuffled out—everyone except little Willy, *sniff-cough*, Runeenoze. "Sir McDoogle?"

I turned to see him at the door. "Oh, hi, Willy."

"Can you help me with my homework now?"

I sighed wearily. "I'm pretty beat at the moment."

"Right." He hacked and wheezed. "Being a superhero can be exhausting work, but—"

"Not now, kid," Wall Street said. "He'll help you *after* the parade."

"Really?" Willy coughed.

"Yeah. Now run along."

"Great!" With that he grinned, turned, and sniffled his way down the hall.

I looked at Wall Street. "What parade?"

"The one the mayor is throwing in your honor."

"The mayor?" I kinda squeaked.

"Yeah, the governor is out of the state."

"The governor?" I majorly croaked.

Wall Street explained. "You're hot stuff now. And when Junior and I are through with you, Wally the Wonder Wimp will be even hotter."

I cleared my throat. "About that name . . ."

"Hey, we tried everything else—Wally the Whacky, Wally the Weird One, Wally the Wombat."

"Wombat? Isn't that a furry creature who lives in Australia?"

"Like I said before . . . we tried *everything*. McDoogle the Mutant, McDoogle the Moron, Mini-Mind McDoogle. But nothing had the right ring for an up-and-coming superhero of your supersize."

I nodded. Once again I recalled God's invitation for me to:

Make the world a better place.

From what I could tell, it was definitely happening. And, with Wall Street's help, a lot sooner than I'd expected . . . or wanted.

"Now, hurry up and get some rest," she said. "We need you well by the time of the parade."

"When's that?" I asked.

She looked at her watch. "About four minutes."

I closed my eyes. Yes sir, some things never change.

Chapter 5

The Plot Sickens . . .

On the Superhero Superparade Scale of 1 to 10, mine was definitely an 11.

At least for the first couple of hours . . .

But by the fifth hour (Wall Street likes long parades), as the people kept cheering and cheering, and I kept waving and waving, it dropped to a 7.6.

By the ninth hour (she *really* likes long parades), we were down to a 6.8. . . .

And by midnight we're talking 4.7 . . . though it quickly dropped to a 0.5 when the blizzard hit.

FUTURE NOTE TO ALL SUPERHEROES: Never do a Superhero Superparade in the middle of January at night—especially if it involves wearing thin superhero tights.

Don't get me wrong. I appreciated the appreciating, but I'd been smiling so much I was afraid my mouth was forever stuck in Perma-Grin. Then there was the boredom factor. Luckily, I'd brought along Ol' Betsy, my faithful laptop. So, instead of letting the parade become a cure for insomnia, I went back to work on my Normal Dude superhero story:

When we last left our notoriously natural and non-novel hero, **Normal Dude**, the author of this little epic was way into overdoing the *fisssowitzzzz*...sound effect.

(You think it was bad before, wait till you see what's coming up.)

Realizing Fast Forward Fiend has infiltrated the entire world with fast-forward remotes, our hero races outside and shouts to his neighbors:

"Friends, Romans, countrymen, lend me your remotes!"

But since nobody is into reading Shakespeare these days, the entire neighborhood steps out onto their porches and shouts, "HUH?!"

"You must give up your fast-forward controls," he yells, "before anything worse happens!"

"No way!" his next-door neighbor shouts.

"Forget it!" his next-to-his-next-door neighbor screams.

"Do these pants make me look fat?" Sister 3 cries.

Doing his best to ignore his sister (something that comes naturally from years of practice), he continues shouting to his neighbors. "You can't just skip through time whenever you want."

"Why not? I'm bored!" his neighbor across the street yells.

"Why not? I hate now!" the next-door neighbor to the neighbor across the street screams.

"Why not? I still have my pimple!" Sister 1 cries.

"Because you'll never enjoy life," Normal Dude explains. "Instead of always looking to the future, you must learn to enjoy the now."

The neighbor behind him yawns. "You're boring me."

The next-door neighbor to the neighbor behind him stretches. "Me, too."

"I forget," Sister 1 says, reaching for the remote, "what does this little button do?"

fisssowitzzzz...

Suddenly, Normal Dude has finished his speech and discovers that he is now walking into his house.

"No!" he shouts, and races back out into the street.

"This is really getting old!" another neighbor (from who knows or cares where) says, reaching for his remote.

fisssowitzzzz...

Suddenly, Normal Dude is in bed.

"No!" he yells as he throws on his clothes and races back out into the street.

"Give us a break!" the neighbor next to the neighbor from who knows or cares where shouts and

*fisssowitzzzz*es

him to the breakfast table.

Again Normal Dude races out into
the street.

"You forgot to put the cap on the
toothpaste!" Sister 2 whines and

*fisssowitzzzz*es

him into the bathroom where he's brushing his teeth before bed.

"Moh *foam-foam-foam* mo!" our hero
yells through a mouthful of toothpaste.

"Mwat mill I *bubble-bubble-bubble*
moo?"

Then, just when it couldn't get any
more confusing:

Ta-da-Daaaa...

the bad-guy music plays. Our hero
looks around but can't find the
viciously vile villain anywhere. Until
he hears Fast Forward Fiend call:

"Over here."

"Mwhere?"

"Right here in front of you, Normal
Dude!"

Our hero turns to the mirror just
as his freaky foe flashes a fabulously

fantastic reflection of frowningness. (Say that with a mouthful of toothpaste.)

"Mast Morward Miend!" our hero foams. "Mis mat moo?"

"Of course, it's me. Didn't you see my fabulously fantastic reflection of frowningness?"

"Mait ma minute. 'Mrowningness' misn't ma mord!"

"I don't care if it's a word. Just rinse and spit so we can get on with the story."

Our hero obeys. Suddenly

fisssowitzzzz . . .

his mouth is once again full of tooth-paste. But instead of brushing before bed, he's brushing after breakfast.

"Mat's mot munny," he shouts and spits, only to be

*fisssowitzzzz*ed

to the evening, where he's brushing again. Then

*fisssowitzzzz*ed

to the morning, then to the

    fisssowitzzzz...

well, you get the picture. And just
when you think this silliness will go
on forever, he's

    *fisssowitzzzz*ed

so far forward that he's run out of
toothpaste!
  Gratefully, Normal Dude spits out
the last of his foam and is preparing
for a normal conversation when—

    fisssowitzzzz...

his mouth is now full of bacon and
eggs, until: *fisssowitzzzz*...now it's a
peanut-butter-and-jelly sandwich,
until: *fisssowitzzzz*...now it's Mom's
macaroni-and-cheese dinner. And so
on, *fisssowitzzzz*, and so forth, *fisssowitzzzz*, it goes as he has to eat meal
after meal, never getting the chance
to empty his mouth.
  Of course, Fast Forward Fiend throws

in his copyrighted, bad-guy

"Moo-hoo-hoo-ha-ha-ha..."

laugh. And, of course, Normal Dude
shouts his required, "Mou'll mever met
maway mith miss!"

Meanwhile, his sisters are having
their own panic attacks with such
insightful observations as: "I'm getting fat from all this food!"

And, "Don't worry, we'll just print
'Goodyear' on your side!"

And then, when this story has de-
generated into total chaos—

"Hey, Wonder Wimp?" Suddenly, someone
was shouting. I looked up from Ol' Betsy. The
good news was, the parade was over. The bad
news was, my life wasn't.

Junior Whiz Kid and Wall Street had picked
me up and were carrying me off the float.

"What's going on?" I asked.

"We have recently decided that combating
unseemly characters is not worthy of our sub-
stantial efforts."

"And in English that means . . ."

"We're going to use you to warn people of world hunger," Wall Street said.

"World hunger?" I asked.

"That is correct. In the time it has taken me to say this single sentence, one person has died of hunger in our world."

"Yes, I remember that from book #25," I said.

"And in the time it takes me to say this second sentence, another person has died."

"That's in there, too!"

"And in the time it takes me to say this third sentence, another person—"

"He gets the idea, Junior."

"Where *are* we going?" I asked.

"Why, back to my laboratory, of course."

"Because . . ."

"Because we must outfit you with even more of my astonishingly cool gizmos to tell people of world hunger."

Wall Street nodded. "And to fill my bank account."

* * * * *

Tap-a-tap-tap. Tap.
Tap-a-tap-tap . . .

I pried open my eyes and looked up to see Bartholomew tap-dancing above me.

"Wh-where am I?" I asked.

"It's *your* dream, Ol' Bean. Where would you like to be?"

I sat up and leaned on my elbow. Looking around, I saw Junior standing nearby.

He was frozen and wearing a surgeon's gown and mask. Beside him was a table full of high-tech junk. On the other side was Wall Street—also in a gown and also frozen.

"Is this an operating room?" I asked.

"I believe so."

"And—"

"You have been knocked out so they can attach more superhero gizmos to you."

"Oh, no," I groaned.

"Oh, yes," he said, grinning.

"And you're back because—"

"I have another message for you."

"Wasn't stopping those bad guys enough?" I asked. "Didn't I help make the world a better enough place by doing that?"

Bartholomew gave one last flurry of

Tap-a-tap-tapping

before he hopped off the table. "Let's see what the Boss says, shall we?" He took off his top hat and reached inside.

As I leaned forward to see, he suddenly pulled out a snorting pink rhinoceros head.

"AUGH!" I cried.

"AUGH!" he agreed.

"What are you doing?" I shouted.

"It's your dream, Wallace, not mine!"

To be honest, the snorting pink rhinoceros head wasn't so bad. Not compared to the rest of the animal as it fought and strained to climb out of the hat!

Of course, Bartholomew did what any angel I dreamed up would do—he dropped the hat and raced around the operating table to hide behind me.

We watched as the cranky rhino finished squeezing out of the hat and arrived in the operating room. Of course, Wall Street and Junior were still frozen and totally oblivious.

And, of course, I wasn't . . . unless you call being "totally oblivious" wanting to crawl under the blanket and scream for your mommy. And I would have, except there was no blanket there. And, as far as I could tell, no mommy.

The weird news was, the rhino didn't charge. The weirder news was, it sprouted little wings and started flapping them.

Bartholomew peeked around me. "I say, Wallace, that is one very strange imagination you have."

"Tell me about it," I sighed as the rhino rose off the floor and started circling around the room.

"I wonder what he wants?" I asked.

"Actually," Bartholomew said, nervously clearing his throat, "he's not a he, he's an *it*."

"An *it*?"

"Yes, a message, remember?"

I looked at him, not understanding.

"Just as you received a message in the form of a pigeon in Mr. Reptenson's class, so you're receiving a message in the form of a rhinoceros."

"No way," I exclaimed. "It's not landing on *my* shoulder!"

He looked at me and shrugged. "It's your imagination."

Before I could answer, the operating table shook with a loud

K-thud.

Ol' Pinky had landed ever so gently (well, as gently as flying rhinos can land) on the table beside me.

"H-h-h-hi there?" I kinda stuttered.

"SNORT!"

it kinda snorted.

"What do I do?" I whispered to Bartholomew.

"I'd reach out and take it."

"Take it! Take it where? It weighs four gazillion tons!"

"It's a message, remember? Just treat it like a message card."

"You mean touch it?" I asked.

"For starters, why not?"

Actually, I could think of a thousand *why nots*. Each and every one of them starting with the phrase: "The reason I'd prefer to keep on living is . . ."

Unfortunately, I only had time to think up two or three hundred before the rhino lowered its horn at me, took a giant breath, and gave another one of its world-famous

*SNORT*s.

Well, it was now or never (though *never* is often my favorite choice in these circumstances). My hands trembling, I reached out to the big boy.

"Nice rhino, rhino, rhino," I said. "Yes, you're a good boy, aren't you?"

It cocked its head and waited until I finally touched its snout. But instead of biting my hand off (or any other body part attached to that hand), it instantly

Poof!

disappeared. Well, not entirely. Instead, he had turned into a note card that gently floated down through the air until it landed in my lap.

I looked at Bartholomew.

"Well, don't just sit there, Ol' Bean. Open it and see what it says."

At first I didn't know what was scarier—dealing with an imaginary rhino or a message from God. But the more I thought about it, the more I realized I had nothing to fear. Hadn't I made the world a better place by capturing those bad guys? Hadn't I wound up in all the newspapers, made all the TV shows? And don't forget that megaparade they just had in my honor.

The way I figured it, I was one very successful success. So, no doubt this would be a thank-you card, or a congratulations card, or maybe even a gift card (hmm, I wonder where God shops).

With a growing smile of satisfaction, I took the card, opened it, and read:

Nice try.
But you missed it by a mile.

Chapter 6

New and Not-So-Improved

"Wally, can you hear me?" The voice was very faint, and I tried my best to ignore it.

Unfortunately, it didn't feel like ignoring me. "Wally?"

I practiced more of my ignoring.

It practiced more of its not-ignoring me. **"WALLY!"**

That's the one that popped open my eyes and shot me up in bed. "What?!"

The good news was, Bartholomew, the rhino, and even the note were gone. The bad news was, Junior Whiz Kid and Wall Street weren't.

"How are you feeling?" Wall Street asked.

"Pas mal," I said. I frowned and tried again. *"Quel est le problème avec ma voix?"*

Wall Street turned to Junior. "What's going on?"

"He is communicating to us in French."

"Français!" I cried.

"Yes, it appears the newly implanted translator is giving us some difficulty." With that, Junior gave the box of buttons on my chest a good

K-thwack!

"How is that?" he asked.

I answered in Spanish. "¿Qué está mal con mi voz?"

K-thwack!

Make that Greek: "Τι κάνει λάθος με τη φωνή μου;"

K-thwack!

"And now?"

Reluctantly, I opened my mouth. Rejoicefully, I was finally speaking English:

"Testing, one, two, three . . ." I shook my head. "Boy, that was weird."

"It's only the beginning," Wall Street said.

"*What?*"

Ignoring me, she asked, "But everything's okay now, right?"

I nodded. "Except I've got this sudden craving for Greek food."

Junior stepped in. "I am afraid there is little time to eat." As he spoke he helped me

creak-groan-squeak

sit up.

"Don't tell me," I sighed. "I'm back to wearing my tin can."

"All right."

"All right what?"

"I will not tell you that you are back to wearing your tin can."

It was an old joke, and I let out the world's second-greatest sigh. (The first-greatest is coming up on page 70.)

Junior continued. "However, I would not fear. I have made some impressive improvements."

I looked down at my superhero body and said, "Well, at least all the scratches and dents are gone."

"We took you to a car-and-body shop," Junior explained.

"And they threw in a wash-and-wax job for free," Wall Street said, beaming.

I nodded, not exactly feeling the same enthusiasm. But I was impressed with all the gizmos and gadgets they'd added . . . like the little monitor on my chest and the box with all the buttons.

Then there were my cool steel legs, not to mention some very neat boots. My favorite, though, was a belt with a cute little **W** on the buckle.

"Outstanding," I said, running my hand over it. "**W** for Wally, right?"

"Actually, it's **W** for Wonder Wimp," Wall Street corrected.

My finger touched a little switch on the side of the buckle.

$$wwWWWWwwwwWWWWWWwww\ldots$$

Well, my finger *had* touched it. But suddenly, my finger disappeared . . . along with every other part of my body!

"What happened?!" I yelled. "Where did I go?!"

"Relax," Wall Street said. "You're still with us."

But where? As far as I could see, I could see nothing. Every part of me had disappeared . . . well, except for my underwear.

"Augh!" I cried, trying to cover up with my hands . . . which, of course, were invisible . . . which, of course, did no good at all!

"Talk about embarrassing!" I cried.

"It could be worse," Wall Street said.

"What could be worse than me having everything invisible except my underwear?!"

"Us having to look at your underwear."

Junior shrugged. "Apparently, we have another malfunction. Wally, will you press that switch on your belt buckle again?"

I nodded and reached for it . . . except I could no longer see where the buckle was, let alone the switch.

"Is this it?" I asked, touching something that caused me to suddenly

$$VVWahhhhhhh\ldots$$

float off the table.

"No, I am afraid that's the lever to your ANTI-GRAVITY FIELD."

I tried again. "What about this?"

flap-flap-flap

"No, those are your PINK RHINO WINGS."

"PINK RHINO WINGS! I thought those were only in my dream!"

"They were, but you transformed them into an image with your DREAM PROJECTOR."

"DREAM PROJECTOR?"

"Any dream you've had may be transformed into a holographic representation of reality by simply pressing the correct button."

"A holographic repre-who?"

"Do not worry, it is merely a picture, nothing real. However, if you would find the correct switch—"

"What switch?" I said. "I don't *see* any switch!"

"Yes, that does appear to be our problem, doesn't it?"

"Wait a minute, I feel something. What about this?"

quora . . . quora . . . quora . . .

"No," Junior cried, "not that—

SPLAWK!

switch!"

Suddenly, I had this desire to make money. Lots and lots of money. And I didn't care what I had to do to make it.

And if that wasn't weird enough, Wall Street started running around the operating room screaming, "This is embarrassing! Turn it off! Turn it off!" as she jumped behind a table to hide.

"What is embarrassing?" Junior asked.

"All you can see is my underwear!" Wall Street cried.

"What are you talking about?" I said. "I'm the one with the underwear."

"But I'm the one feeling it!" she shouted. "Turn it off, turn it off!"

Junior turned to me and explained. "You hit the switch to the EMOTION EXCHANGER."

"The what—"

"Once it is activated, you exchange feelings with the person you last looked at."

I nodded, starting to get it. "That's why Wall Street is so embarrassed and I'm feeling so greedy?"

"Precisely."

"Please!" Wall Street cried. "Turn it off!"

I wanted to help her, but at the same time I couldn't stop thinking about all the money I could make.

"Turn it off, Wally! Turn it off!"

"How much will you pay me?" I asked.

"I'll give you one-half of all I make! Please, this is so embarrassing!"

One-half sounded good, but I was greedy for more. "Make it a fourth, and we have a deal." (I was never great at fractions.)

"Yes, yes. Whatever you say, just turn it off!"

SPLAWK!

quora . . . quora . . . quora . . .

Wall Street and I both shook our heads.

"How do you feel now?" Junior asked me.

I looked down at my floating underwear. "Embarrassed."

"Perfect." He turned to Wall Street. "And you?"

"I wonder how much money we can make off this thing." Then, shuddering, she added, "That was awful!"

"Welcome to my world," I said.

She shuddered again. "It was . . . I can't think of the word. . . ."

"Incredible?" I offered.

"Exactly! What an incredible world!" Suddenly, her eyes lit up. "Hey, that'd be a cool title for a book series. The Incredible Worlds of . . . of . . ."

"Wally McDoogle?" I suggested.

"No, that'll never sell. But . . . The Incredible Worlds of Wonder Wimp! Now there's a title!"

Junior interrupted. "As much as I find this discussion stimulating, we should be going. Every second wasted is another person starving."

Wall Street nodded. "And another dollar slipping out of my hands."

They turned and started toward the door.

"Wait a minute!" I said. "What about me in this floating underwear? And what about all these other switches and gizmos? What do they do?"

"You'll just have to wait and see," Wall Street said. "Unless you want to pay me $19.95 for the instruction booklet."

I reached into my pockets to see what money I had. A good idea, except tin-can bodies seldom have pockets.

"I'm broke," I said.

"Then I guess you'll just have to wait. . . ."

Chapter 7
Late-Breaking News

We borrowed a topcoat from Junior's dad's closet and threw it on me. It was better than just underwear, but the headless look was a little tacky (and a lot freaky), so we grabbed a ski mask and pulled it down over my face. I knew it made me look like a bad guy, but I figured it was better to look like a bad guy than a no guy.

Meanwhile, Wall Street called a taxi.

"Where are we going?" I asked as we climbed in.

"WACK-O TV," Wall Street explained.

"Why?"

"In order to warn people about world hunger, we have to tell them about world hunger."

"So, we're going to tell one of their reporters?" I asked.

"Actually, *you're* going to be one of their reporters," Junior said.

"I'll WHAT?!"

"Relax," Wall Street said. "You'll just sneak into the studio, climb into the news anchor's chair, and give the report."

"I'll WHAT?!"

Junior explained. "I attempted to reason with them. I even asked them to do a special report about the hungry."

"And?"

"And they said people were more interested in watching reality shows."

"What could be more real than people starving?" I asked.

"He means *real* reality," Wall Street said. "Like silly people being dared to do silly things, or date silly people, or make and wear silly clothes."

I frowned. "But that's so . . . so . . ."

"Silly?" Wall Street offered.

I nodded.

"Which is why you'll be going on TV to tell them what's really real."

"I'll WHAT?!" (*Hey, when you find a good phrase, it doesn't hurt to wear it out.*)

We arrived at the station, climbed out of the taxi, and slipped into the lobby. All the time I kept trying to reason with the two of them. "I can't go on TV, I get tongue-tied just giving book reports in front of our class."

"This will be an entirely different experience," Junior assured me as we dropped to our knees and snuck past the receptionist's desk toward the studio doors.

"Yeah," Wall Street whispered. "You won't be seen by a bunch of dopey kids."

"That's a relief," I sighed.

"You'll be seen by *millions* of them . . . and their parents, too."

"I'll mwat?!" (That was supposed to be another "I'll WHAT?!" but they managed to cover my mouth before I finished.) When they were sure I was under control, they removed their hands, and we continued toward the studio doors. Once we arrived, we pushed them open and entered.

The place was darker than a piece of licorice stuck to a black cat during an eclipse in the middle of the night.

TRANSLATION: It was dark.

Except for the empty newsdesk. It was lit up brighter than a vanilla shake dumped on a white cat during a snowstorm in the middle of— well, you get the picture.

Once inside, we stood up and looked around.

The good news was, nobody was there. The bad news was, we were.

"I r-r-really don't think I can d-d-do this," I stuttered.

"Wally, you must relax."

"B-b-but—"

"Actually, Wall Street was quite incorrect when she said you'd be seen by millions," Junior said.

"Sh-sh-she was?"

"Yes. In reality, you won't be seen by *anyone*."

"I won't?"

"That is correct," he said as he removed my coat and stood on a chair to take off my ski mask. "All those millions of viewers will see is your underwear."

(For some reason this gave me little comfort.)

Once we arrived at the newsdesk, I looked at Wall Street, and she looked at me.

I turned to look at Junior, and he turned to look at me.

Finally, with the world's biggest sigh (hey, I told you it was coming), I stepped around the desk and plopped into the chair. To be honest, it felt good to be hiding behind the desk. Well, actually, it felt good to have my underwear hiding behind the desk. Maybe things wouldn't be so bad after all.

"How'd you kids get in here?!" a voice shouted.

We spun around to see some old janitor. He'd

been mopping in the back of the room, but now he was coming at us.

"Well, hello there," Junior politely said.

"What are you doing?" he impolitely growled.

"We have come to utilize your Electronic Optical Image Enhancer."

"My *what?!*"

"Your TV cameras," Wall Street explained.

Junior glanced toward me and continued. "Particularly the one directly in front of the newsdesk with the little green switch on the side."

I frowned, not understanding what he was saying.

Janitor Man frowned and didn't particularly care. Instead, he grabbed both Junior and Wall Street by the arms. "You two don't belong here."

But Junior wasn't finished. Still looking in my direction, he continued, "The green switch, which when clicked to its upright position turns on the camera and sends the signal to the control booth, which then broadcasts it to the entire region."

"That's enough!" Janitor Man pulled them toward the door. "You two skedaddle, 'fore I call the cops."

"Well, all right then," Junior said. "I just hope that camera does not switch on by itself."

"Yeah, right," Janitor Man said as he pushed open the doors and threw my friends out. "Now get."

Once they were gone, he turned back to the newsdesk and squinted.

I froze. I was pretty sure he couldn't see me, but he was sure seeing something.

He started toward me.

My heart began

thump-thump-thumping.

I glanced down. My underwear was perfectly hidden, but he kept right on coming, and my heart kept right on

thump-thump-thumping.

Finally, he arrived and slowed to a stop. He was less than four feet from me. And then, just when I was about to jump up and shout, "All right, you got me, I'm the one you can't see in the tin suit with all the gizmos including a giant **W** for a belt buckle that has made me invisible, except for my underwear, that you see floating before you!" Anyway, just before I got around to sharing that little tidbit of info, he reached down and grabbed my topcoat and ski mask that had been left on the desk.

"Silly kids," he muttered as he turned and headed back across the room to his mop and bucket.

I breathed a sigh of relief and closed my eyes. What had Junior been talking about—cameras and green switches and control booths? Suddenly, my eyes popped back open and I knew. Unfortunately, I knew.

I was sitting at a newsdesk ten feet in front of a camera. According to Junior, all I had to do was switch a little green switch on the side and we would be broadcasting.

Of course, a huge part of me didn't want to. But a huger part knew I had to. Somebody had to tell everyone about the hungry. Someone had to be the hero and tell the world. Once again, my heart returned to its favorite pastime of

thump-thump-thumping.

Unfortunately, my brain thought it would join in with some

think . . . thinking . . . thinking

(never a good sign . . . at least in these stories).

Still, wasn't I in a position to do exactly what Bartholomew had asked? By turning on that camera and broadcasting, wouldn't I be making the world a better place?

I looked up and stared at the camera.

Of course, I couldn't exactly get up and stroll over to turn it on. (Well, I could, but I hear old-guy janitors have a tendency to have heart attacks whenever they see underwear floating across rooms.)

There had to be another way.

Unfortunately, my brain was still

think-think-thinking,

which meant I eventually came up with a plan.

First, I tried moving my newly installed EXTENDO ARM (the very one Junior had destroyed half a city block with). And, sure enough, just like old times, it

K-ZIIIING!

shot out and

K-Rash!ed

into the far wall at the other end of the studio.

Realizing I might have stretched it a bit too far, I pulled back the arm until it

K-Bamb!

hit my desk. This, of course, was interrupted by expected screams such as: "AUGH! A GHOST! A GHOST!" and the usual, scared-out-of-their-mind shrieks that janitors often make as they stumble over their

K-Rash
glug-glug-glug

mop and bucket while running out of studios for their lives.

But I paid little attention. I was too busy concentrating on my EXTENDO ARM. Ever so gently I

k-zing . . . . . . k-zing . . . . . . k-zing . . . . . .

moved it out toward the camera.

Finally, with a few more k-*zing*ings (and a minimal amount of *K-rash*ings), I reached the little green switch. I gave it one little

K-lick!

Suddenly, a red light on top of the camera popped on.

And, just as suddenly, a light in the control

booth upstairs came on. Junior had broken in. I
could see him dashing to the control board.
Immediately, he began punching buttons, dial-
ing dials, and knobbing knobs.

Finally, he looked at me and gave me the
thumbs-up. It was now or never. And though
never always seems like a better choice, I knew
it was time, once again, to be a superhero.

Chapter 8

More Superheroics

Now was my chance—the opportunity to use all of my stupendous superhero powers for the good of the world.

I reached into my pocket to pull out the speech I should have written . . . which I didn't . . . which was okay because, as you remember, metal suits don't have pockets anyway.

Once again my heart began

thump-thump-thumping

louder than the speaker in some rapper's car.

I looked at the camera.

It looked at me.

My eyes squinted.

Its red light glowed.

Finally, after a little prayer to God (and a promise to start treating my little sister better if He let me live), I cleared my throat and began:

"*Gasp-gasp. Wheeze-wheeze. Gasp-wheeze . . . wheeze-gasp.*"

Try as I might, no words would come! It's not that I was camera-shy. I was camera-*horrified*. All I could do was gasp and try to catch my breath. The good news was, I was able to get enough air to breathe. The bad news was, I didn't get enough to sound like a human being (or any other intelligent life form).

I glanced up at the control booth. Junior motioned for me to take deeper breaths. So, with nothing else better to do than faint from hyperventilating, I took some deeper *gasps* and *wheezes* and tried again.

"Hi, there. I'm Wally McDoogle . . ."

My voice was about ten octaves higher than normal, but at least I had one. I cleared my throat and continued:

"People are starving."

There. Done. I was brilliant, if I do say so myself. I had made my point, and now it was time to go.

Well, not exactly . . .

Junior was up in the booth waving for me to go on. He looked so concerned and desperate, and we had worked so hard to get here, that I took another breath and continued:

"And not just a few people. I'm talking a thousand people every hour. That's 24,000 people a day dying of hunger!"

I noticed the door to the control booth flying open and a couple of guys in suits running toward Junior. I didn't have much time.

"I know it'd be a lot more fun watching beautiful shows with beautiful actors lost on beautiful islands, or investigating how other beautiful actors are killed, or chasing beautiful actor bad guys, but . . . 24,000 lives a day, people!"

Up in the booth the suits had wrestled Junior to the ground. I talked faster.

"And we have enough food to feed everyone. In fact, we produce four and a half pounds of food each day for every man, woman, and child in the world! But they're not getting it, because we're too lazy or greedy or just don't care, or—"

KA-ZOOOOooo . . .

Suddenly, the light on the camera went out. The broadcast was done. But that was okay. I'd said what had to be said.

We had actually succeeded!

Proudly, I rose from the newsdesk. With head held high, I crossed the studio floor and headed out the doors with the greatest-possible

dignity . . . well, with as much dignity as floating underwear can have.

* * * * *

Yes sir, it was one satisfying experience
telling people about world hunger. It was also
pretty exhausting. So, on the way home in the
taxi with Wall Street (Junior's mode of trans-
portation was in the back of a police car), I
relaxed and got back to my superhero story.

The only problem was, I didn't have Ol'
Betsy.

But I did have a pretty good imagination. So,
I sat back, closed my eyes, and did what I know
best. . . .

When we last left Normal Dude, Fast
Forward Fiend was making people zip
through time faster than winter break
flies by at Christmas. Worse than
that, Fast Forward Fiend was only stopping at mealtimes—a nice idea if you
like pigging out...not so nice if you
hate being a 3,000-pound pig. I don't
want to say people are getting fat and
bulging out all over the place, but

suddenly the post office is giving everyone their own separate zip codes.

Once again our heroically handsome, though grossly overweight, hero tries to reason with the fiendish foe. "Please, *chew-chew*, you must stop fast-forwarding us, *swallow-swallow,* through time, *burp-BURP!*"

But Fast Forward Fiend is too busy opening health fitness centers and Fat Watchers programs to pay much attention.

Suddenly, in a fleeting thought (which is as long as any thought stays in our hero's head), Normal Dude leaps up from the dinner table and

fisssowitzzzz...

Make that, he leaps up from the breakfast table and

fisssowitzzzz...

All right already. He leaps up from any table and starts walking backward.

"What are you doing?" Sister 3 demands. "And by the way, you don't mind if I finish up your hot cakes—

fisssowitzzzz...

er, sandwiches—

fisssowitzzzz...

er, steak dinner, do you?"

Normal Dude doesn't answer. Instead, he just keeps getting up from the table and walking backward...until he makes it all the way up the stairs and into the bathroom where he last spoke to Fast Forward Fiend.

He looks into the mirror and shouts, "!dneiF drawroF tsaF"

There is no answer and so he tries again: "?ereht uoy era ,dneiF drawroF tsaF"

Suddenly, Fast Forward Fiend appears in the mirror. "What? I can't understand what you're saying!"

".rehtien eM" Normal Dude shrugs and begins walking backward out of the bathroom.

"Wait a minute, stop!" Fast Forward Fiend shouts.

But Normal Dude just keeps on walking backward.

"You can't do that!"

"?ton yhW" Normal Dude asks as he continues...until Fast Forward Fiend panics and presses his

fisssowitzzzz...

remote.

It's a new day, and Normal Dude once again stands in front of the mirror. But once again he starts walking backward until

fisssowitzzzz...

it's another new day as he starts walking backward again.

"What's going on?!" Fast Forward Fiend shouts.

"?naem uoy od tahW" Normal Dude says as he continues walking backward.

fisssowitzzzz...

"I distinctly made the remotes to only have a fast-forward function. What fancy-schmancy superhero gizmo do you have that puts you into reverse?!"

".em toG" Normal Dude resumes walking backward.

fisssowitzzzz...

"I'm the bad guy! Bad guys win
through cheating and fancy gizmos!"
Normal Dude resumes walking backward. "?oS"

fisssowitzzzz...

"So, you're the great Normal Dude!
You're supposed to win through honesty
and brainpower! Not fancy gizmos!"
Normal Dude shrugs and resumes
walking backward.
And how is he able to do this, you ask?
(You are asking, right?)
"I know I am," Fast Forward Fiend
says.
Sorry. This is only for my readers
to know. Now stand over there in that
corner and stop looking over my
shoulder.
"Oh, all right," the bad guy says
as he slinks over to the corner.

I return to my story:

The reason he can do all that back-ward stuff is simple. He's merely pretending to walk and talk backward.

"He's what?"

I open my eyes: **Get back in that corner!**

"You don't have to yell," Fast Forward Fiend says as he reaches for his remote and

fisssowitzzzz...

Suddenly, there's a

*knock-knock-knock*ing

at the front door.

"I'll get it!" Sister 1, 2, or 3 screeches.

Normal Dude starts down the stairs backward when Fast Forward Fiend bursts into the house and shouts, "All right, Dude. I don't know what you have, but we're going to duke it out right now!"

And then, just when you think we've come to the obligatory fight scene of this story—

"Uh-oh," Wall Street said, jabbing me in the ribs and pulling me away from my story. "Don't look now." (Which, of course, meant I had to.)

I turned to the window as we pulled up to my house. There were about a thousand bazillion angry people marching around it. (Okay, I'm exaggerating—more like a thousand *gazillion,* but they were still pretty angry.)

Some were shouting, others were holding picket signs with such clever slogans as:

Entertainment Not Reality!

Let the starving feed themselves!

Stop annoying ME with their problems!

And finally, the ever-popular . . .

Tell the starving to get their own TV channel!

"What's going on?" I asked.

"Looks like they weren't thrilled about you interrupting their TV shows," she said.

"But . . . they have to know!"

She looked out the window. "You want to tell them that?"

I swallowed. "What do you think they want to do to me?"

"There's only one way to find out." Wall Street reached for her door.

Before I had a chance to take a deep breath for bravery (or at least drop to the floor and beg her to stop), Wall Street opened the door, and the people pushed forward.

The good news was, I was still invisible.

"Where is he?" someone shouted.

At first, Wall Street played ignorant. "Who?"

"You know who! That terrible creep!"

"He's destroyed our lives by making us watch reality!" another shouted.

"That's right!" a third said, sobbing. "Now I'll never know who won on *Cockroach Eating Cookout!*"

"Or *Extreme Manicure Makeover!*"

"Or see the end to *Lawyers in Luxury!*"

"Where is he?" they repeated. "Where is Wally McDoogle?"

And Wall Street, being the thoughtful and dedicated friend she is, did what any thoughtful and dedicated friend would do. She turned toward my underwear, pointed, and shouted: "THERE HE IS!"

Good ol' Wall Street. Faster than you can say "Benedict Arnold," they raced around to my side of the car and yanked me out. And, since they couldn't exactly see what part of me to yank, they yanked

"AUGHHHH!"

every part. Arms, legs, toes, you name it—if it was connected to some part of my body, they tried disconnecting it from my body.

Soon, they had me out of the car and hoisted above their heads. But since carrying invisible people isn't always the easiest (in some states you have to take a special test for it), they managed to drop me on my

K-Thud

head more times

K-Thud K-Thud

than I could

K-Thud K-Thud K-Thud K-Thud K-Thud
K-Thud K-Thud K-Thud K-Thud K-Thud
K-Thud K-Thud K-Thud K-Thud K-Thud

K-Thud K-Thud K-Thud K-Thud K-Thud
K-Thud K-Thud K-Thud K-Thud K-Thud

count.

The good news was, all that *K-Thud*ding managed to shake the invisible switch on my belt until it finally

wwW*W*wwwwwwwwW*W*Wwww.

shut off.

The bad news was, now everyone could clearly see which part of my body they were tearing apart.

I couldn't believe it. How could people be so upset about my interrupting their TV shows—especially when it meant telling them about others who were starving to death?

"Please!" I yelled. "I was only trying to let you know there are suffering people!"

"Yes," a beautiful, model-type lady said as she wiped her eyes. "You taught me all about suffering."

"I did?" I said, pleased that someone had listened to me.

She nodded, trying to hold back her tears. "I was watching *Greed TV* where they had a sale on Automatic Eyebrow-Pluckers."

"And?" I asked hopefully.

"And you came on and"—she broke into hysterical sobbing—"and I never got to order it!"

Her emotional pain sent the crowd into a fury.

"PEOPLE! PEOPLE!"

I turned to see Wall Street climbing out of the car. It looked like she'd finally come to her senses—like she was actually going to help me.

(Hey, everyone needs to dream.)

"I UNDERSTAND THE PAIN WALLY HAS CAUSED YOU!" she yelled.

"Shout, shout! Grumble, grumble! Complain, complain!" the people shouted, grumbled, and complained.

"AND I'M GOING TO MAKE IT UP TO EACH AND EVERY ONE OF YOU!"

"Yeah, yeah? Really, really? Is she kidding?"

"JUST TELL ME HOW MUCH YOU SUFFERED, AND I'LL PAY YOU FOR ALL THE DAMAGES!"

"Yea, yea! Cheer, cheer! Yippee, Yippee!"

I couldn't believe my ears. Wall Street was finally coming around. Maybe it was all the talk about helping the hungry. Maybe she'd finally stopped being so greedy.

"That's great!" I called to her. "I'm so proud of you."

She beamed. "Thanks. Of course, there will be a slight interest-and-handling fee."

"How much?" I asked.

"For every dollar I pay out, you'll pay me back seven."

With that bit of cheery news, the crowd finally set me

K-thunk

down.

As I was dragging myself up the porch steps toward the house I heard:

"Sir McDoogle, *sniff-sniff*, Sir Mc, *cough-cough*, Doogle?"

I looked up to see little Willy Runeenoze standing above me. "Can you help me with my homework now?"

"I'm a little busy," I said. "Think you can catch me tomorrow?"

"Sure, *hack-hack*, thing." He grinned, then he went wheezing off.

Finally, I dragged my superhero body into the house. It would be great to have Mom and Dad there to comfort me. It would have been greater if they weren't standing in line to get their money from Wall Street.

So, doing my best not to cry (metal superhero

bodies tend to rust), I dragged myself up the stairs and plopped into bed to get some sleep.

Actually, it wasn't the sleep I was interested in. It was the dream. At least Bartholomew would appreciate my work.

And, more important . . . so would God.

Chapter 9

In Your Dreams . . . (or Not)

"Hello . . . *ello* . . . *ello* . . ." I shouted into the darkness. "Can anybody . . . *ody* . . . *ody* hear me . . . *me* . . . *me* . . . ?"

Nobody answered.

I paused a minute and thought, "How strange . . . *ange* . . . *ange*. Hey, wait a minute . . . *ute* . . . *ute*. . . . These are just thoughts . . . *oughts* . . . *oughts*. Thoughts don't have echoes . . . *oes* . . . *oes*. . . . Do they . . . *ey* . . . *ey* . . . ?"

That's when I realized I wasn't in reality, but in one of my "dreams . . . *eams* . . . *eams*. . . ."

"Oh, knock it off . . . *off* . . . *off* . . . ," I thought.

"Sorry . . . *orry* . . . *orry* . . . ," I thought back.

Anyway, if I was back in dreamland, that meant I ought to be able to talk to Bartholomew, right? The only problem was, Ol' Bart wasn't anywhere to be seen. At least not in this dark void full of echoes . . . *oes* . . . *oes*. . . .

I closed my eyes (a neat trick since they tend
to be closed when you're dreaming, anyway) and
pictured myself back in Reptile Man's class.
When I reopened them, sure enough, there I
was, sitting at my desk surrounded by the same
bored kids listening to the same boring teacher.

But there was no Bartholomew. No white
tux. No top hat. And no *tap-a-tap-tap. Tap. Tap-
a-tap-tap* . . .

I tried again and closed my eyes. This time I
pictured myself in the operating room with the
flying rhino *SNORT*ing away.

Again, there was nothing. Except . . . there, on
the operating table beside me, sat Bartholomew's
top hat. Of course, I wasn't crazy about reaching
inside it, but since he wasn't around and that's
where the notes always came from, I figured I
didn't have much choice.

So, with trembling hands, and more than a
few trembling prayers, I reached inside to find
. . . a folded piece of paper. I nervously pulled it
out, grateful it didn't turn into a fire-breathing
dragon, a boy-eating T. rex, or any of the usual
stuff I dream up.

I had no idea what it would say. I had succeeded in stopping those bank robbers, but
apparently I'd not done what God wanted.

Would the same thing be true with telling

the people about world hunger? I mean, despite
the embarrassments, catastrophes, embarrassments, mishaps, and, of course, embarrassments,
I *had* succeeded. True, not everyone wanted to
hear, but that wasn't the point. I had succeeded
in telling them.

So, with growing anticipation and excite-
ment, I unfolded the note and read:

Out to Lunch

What?! After all I'd done?! After all I'd been
through?!

I glanced back at the paper. Only then did I
notice the fine print in the bottom-right corner.
It read:

(over)

The message was on the paper's other side.
Bartholomew must have stepped out for lunch
and left it. I quickly flipped the paper over and
in one breathless moment read:

You still don't get it, do you?

Get it? Get what? What more could I do?! I
had used my superhero powers to the max, and

I had succeeded! So, what was the problem? I know it's not cool to be mad at God, but I was getting a little steamed. I was just about to crumple up the paper and toss it when I noticed the fine print at the bottom right-hand corner of this side. It also read:

(over)

It made no sense. I'd just read the other side. But with nothing else better to do, I flipped the paper over to read an entirely different message:

> *I have given you several opportunities*
> *to make the world a better place,*
> *and you keep getting it wrong.*

Getting it wrong?! I'd done everything I could! What more did He want?

Again, I started to crumple the note, and again I noticed another set of words in the lower right-hand corner.

(over again, please)

This was getting ridiculous. I flipped the paper and read:

You're looking in the wrong place.

(over—

last time,

I promise)

I shook my head in frustration. I had tried. I had done everything He had told me to do! I flipped the paper to read:

Not quite.

* * * * *

I woke up the next morning, and fortunately found an extra set of directions to my superhero suit (they were in the waistband, in case you ever buy one), and studied every word. I still had time. I was going to do what God had asked, and I was going to do it today!

Without showering (superhero suits have a tendency to rust), I reached to the keypad on my chest, punched in the code for my BALLISTIC ROCKET BOOTS (#357 if you're interested) and

K-Whooshed

off to make the world a better place.

I wasn't sure what I would find, but like Bartholomew had said, I figured God would show me something. Actually, it might have been a few too many somethings. . . .

First, there was the ever-popular and always-expected

RUNAWAY SCHOOL BUS.

The way it roared down the mountain road at a thousand miles an hour, completely out of control, while

K-scraping and K-bambing

into the guardrail told me there might be a problem. I was even more certain when my ULTRAFREQUENCY HEADSET (#359) heard the driver shouting:

"HELP ME! HELP ME! THERE MIGHT BE A PROBLEM!"

Spiraling past a bird that looked so concerned I figured it had read some of my adventures, I dropped down in front of the school bus just seconds before it arrived.

Pressing #401 (you're writing these down for future reference, right?), my EXTENDO CLEATS extended from my boots and into the ground.

These, of course, would prevent me from sliding as I stuck out my titanium arms and stopped the bus from . . .

K-SMASH!
K-SNAP!

(Okay, maybe I didn't exactly stop it. And okay, maybe EXTENDO CLEATS snap off a lot easier than you'd expect.) But the good news was, the bus only dragged me two or three hundred yards before it flung me aside and I

roll-roll-rolled

into a giant maple . . . or elm . . . or sycamore. (It's hard distinguishing vegetation when you're smashing major body parts.)

Fortunately, I didn't die (though I could sure have used an aspirin or two). Instead, my SPRING-LOADED LEGS (#403) shot me back to my feet just as my EXTENDO ARMS (#331) shot backward and grabbed the bus's back bumper. They hung on until they brought the bus to a

SKIIIIIIIIIDDing

stop.

The bus door opened, and a hundred hysterical kids ran out screaming, "Yippee! We're going to miss first period!"

Of course, the bus driver wanted to thank me (and probably get the phone number for ordering his own superhero suit with the *new-and-improved* EXTENDO CLEATS), but I had other matters to tend to.

Up above us, my SUPER-KEEN-O-VISION GOGGLES (#423) saw a jet airliner. A bolt of lightning had sheered off one of its wings, and it was dropping from the sky faster than my grades when I gave up studying for Lent.

So, firing up my boots and turning on my ANTI-LIGHTNING GENERATOR (#104—good for removing unsightly static cling, in both the air and your underwear), I managed to grab the airliner from below and gently brought it down to the ground.

After a free in-flight snack and a complimentary movie headset, I smelled something burning. Punching up my SUPER-SNOOPER SMOKE SMELLER (sorry, this is a special-order item that is not listed on standard superhero suit keypads), I smelled a burning building.

I took off and flew downtown to join the fire department in trying to save a few more hundred lives. At first it was the usual

K-whooshing

up and pulling people out the windows of burning rooms, then

K-whooshing

down with them clinging to me while sobbing, "Oh, thank you, Wonder Wimp, thank you" (as I pleaded with them to back off on the tears because of the rust factor).

Things were going pretty good until the fire department suddenly ran out of water. (I'm not sure of the details—something about the mayor forgetting to pay the water bill.)

In desperation, the firemen turned to me. "Wonder Wimp, what can we do?"

Of course, I was my usual clueless self, until I pulled out the instruction booklet and gave it a quick review. And there, right in the appendix (which until then I'd thought was a part of the human body), I found the answer.

"Quick," I shouted, "everybody, gather around!" I punched in #825, #834, and #913.

Instantly, a giant hose nozzle shot out of my left arm. Instantlier (don't try that word in English class), the other end of the hose shot out of my right arm with a giant funnel attached to it.

"What is it?!" everyone shouted.

"It's the SUPERECONO SALIVA MULTIPLIA!"

"The what?"

"No time to explain. Just come to the funnel here and spit into it. Spit into it as much as you can, and the SALIVA MULTIPLIA will do the rest."

"But *Multiplia* is not even a word!" they complained.

"I know," I said. "It was invented by some rap artist. But you're going to have to trust me on this."

Reluctantly, they agreed and began to

spit, spit, spit, spit

then

spit, spit, spit, spit, spit, spit, spit, spit, spit,
spit, spit, spit, spit, spit, spit, spit, spit, spit,
spit, spit, spit, spit, spit, spit, spit, spit, spit,
spit, spit, spit, spit, spit, spit, spit, spit, spit

some more.

Soon, the SALIVA MULTIPLIA kicked in and began replicating the structure of their saliva's DNA, not to mention multiplying the subatomic particles within the H_2O compound, creating, as you've already figured out . . . more saliva. (If you haven't already figured it out, then you're not taking enough college biology courses.)

Within seconds, thousands of gallons shot out the nozzle of my left arm. Soon the entire building was soaked and the fire was out. And—other than a few folks complaining about having to take showers, or threatening to send me their dry-cleaning bills (firemen's spit isn't as attractive as you might think)—most of them seemed grateful.

But talk about exhausting. I was bushed. It had been a long day, and I was more beat than a giant piñata on Cinco de Mayo.

I arrived at my house and staggered up the stairs. I had done everything I could. I had tried everything. And if I hadn't succeeded in what God wanted by now, I never would. So, after a long hot shower (rust or no rust, those folks were right about the spit), I crawled into bed hoping for another dream and praying that I'd finally gotten it right.

Fortunately, we don't always get what we pray for. . . .

Chapter 10

Wrapping Up

I woke up the next morning without having a single dream. Talk about disappointing. I didn't hear from God; I didn't hear from Bartholomew; I didn't hear from anyone.

Well, except for somebody downstairs trying to wear out our

> *ding-dong* . . .
> *ding-dong, ding-dong*

doorbell.

It was Saturday. That always meant Dad had grabbed his clubs and was beating up golf balls, Mom had grabbed her coupons and was saving us into the poorhouse, and my brothers and little sister would be sleeping until sometime next week.

Ding-dong . . .
ding-dong, ding-dong.

"All right already!" I rolled out of bed and

*K-reak*ed
and
*K-squeak*ed

my rusting superhero suit down the stairs.

Even before I reached the door, I promised myself that I'd have Junior cut me out of the tin can today. Enough was enough.

I was done. Finished.

I had tried over and over again, but no matter how hard I tried, no matter what superhero powers I used, I had somehow failed. No matter what I did, no matter how I succeeded in saving the day, I just couldn't find what God wanted me to do. Whatever He had in mind, I wasn't strong enough, or smart enough, or superhero enough to pull it off.

Ding-dong . . .
ding-dong, ding-dong.

Finally, I arrived at the door and opened it.
"Hi, Sir, *sniff-sniff,* McDoogle." It was little

Willy Runeenoze. "I thought we should get an early start, I mean, with so much fun stuff to, *cough-cough,* cover."

"Fun stuff?"

"Remember, you said, *hack-hack,* when you were done saving the world you'd, *AH-CHOO!* help me with diagramming sentences and all my other homework?"

"Oh, that fun stuff."

"Are you finished yet?" he asked. "Saving the world, I mean?"

"Oh, I'm finished all right," I said. "In more ways than you know."

With that bit of cheery news, I opened the door wider and let him in . . . along with his shopping cart full of books.

"Are all these . . . yours?" I asked.

"Yeah," he wheezed. "I've got a little catching up to do."

So, with a heavy sigh, I directed him toward the kitchen table. Of course, it was a little embarrassing, going from World Class Superhero to World Class Superloser. But now that I was done trying to save the world, I needed to find another title.

And so we began. . . .

To be honest, Willy wasn't the brightest candle on the cake. To be even more honest, I wasn't sure he'd even been invited to the party. But I could see the little *sneezing-wheezing* machine trying, and that was good enough for me.

To pass the time (and use my computer screen as a shield against flying germs), I pulled out Ol' Betsy. Whenever Willy came across tough problems that involved new and mysterious tools for him to use (like dictionaries or multiplication tables), I'd turn him loose to explore them while I worked on my superhero story—hoping my fantasy version would turn out better than my real life. . . .

When we last left Normal Dude and Fast Forward Fiend, they were beginning the obligatory fight scene that always happens at the end of these stories. Of course, it would involve plenty more

*fisssowitzzzz*es

and more of Normal Dude's faking him out by talking siht ekil drawkcab.

"What?" Fast Forward Fiend demands.

".siht ekil drawkcaB"

"Oh, yeah, well take this!"

fisssowitzzzz...

   But Dude is unphased and counters with
"H
 o
 w

'b
 o
 u
 t

 t
 h
 i
s?" he asks vertically.
  "Vertically!?" the bad boy cries.
"How can anyone talk vertically?!"

fisssowitzzzz...

"O
  r

    t
   h
    i
      s?" our hero asks diagonally.

"Please!" Fast Forward Fiend cries. "This is insanity. We can't go on like this!"

"W   h   n   t?" our hero asks randomly.
o
y

"Because we're running out of pages in this book, that's why!" Fast Forward Fiend shouts.

Finally, with the logic and sympathy that all superheroes have, Normal Dude clears his throat and begins to talk normally: "Would you please holster that remote of yours so we can talk?"

"But how can I beat you without my gizmo?"

"We'll just have to settle our differences normally by discussing them."

"But it's been so long....I'm not sure I can remember what normal is," Fast Forward Fiend says.

"Exactly," Normal Dude agrees. "Don't you see what's happening? By refusing to live in the now, you're missing everything normal."

"But I'm getting to tomorrow."

"Without living today. Don't you get it? Right now, this moment, can be just as fun or even better...if you take the time to live it."

Fast Forward Fiend scowls, scratching his head.

Normal Dude continues. "Instead of always racing ahead to the next moment, try enjoying this one. And then, when it's done, you can go to the next moment naturally."

"But that's so...so—"

"Normal?" Normal Dude asks.

"Exactly."

"But isn't that how God usually does things?"

"You mean normally?" Fast Forward Fiend asks.

"Yes."

"Hmm," Fast Forward Fiend hmms. "Maybe we can sit down over some hot chocolate somewhere and talk about this."

"Sounds good to me."

"Great. Let me *fisssowitzzzz* us so we're already there and—"

"No, that's okay," Normal Dude says. "I'd rather take my time and enjoy the moments getting there."

"What a novel concept," Fast Forward
Fiend says. "I suppose I can give that
a try."

And so, as the music begins and the
credits roll, the two head off into the
sunset to find some hot chocolate while
discussing how God wants us to go
through time totally and completely—

"Normal?" Fast Forward Fiend asks.

Our hero nods. "That's right. How'd
you know?"

"I read ahead to the next paragraph."

Normal Dude smiles. "But it's true.
How much happier we all would be if we
would live each moment for what it
is...enjoying every second at the
speed God wants us to live it...totally
and completely...

(music swells to BIG finish)

normal."

I stared at the screen. It was obviously one
of my cheesier endings (but the best I could do
with rusting fingers). Suddenly, to my surprise,
more writing appeared:

That's so true, Wally.

My eyes widened. Then I realized that I must have dozed off and was dreaming—which explained why even more words appeared on the screen:

> *Your work catching those bank robbers*
> *was great (and I enjoyed the giggles).*

I blinked and read more.

> *And I really liked your telling people*
> *about world hunger (even though the*
> *underwear stuff was weird).*

I fidgeted and kept reading.

All those other things were thoughtful, too, but . . .

I frowned, knowing He'd say they weren't what He wanted.

> *That's right.*
> *I don't need you in silly superhero suits*
> *with silly superhero gizmos. I just need you to be*
> *your normal, everyday self . . . kind of like*
> *this story you've been writing.*

But how can I help You by being normal? I thought.

*Normal is how I created you, and
normal is how I expect you to help.*

*I don't . . . understand. You said You'd show
me how to make the world a better place, but
You never showed me a thing.*

*That's because you weren't paying attention.
Look around at what you can do normally, Wally.*

But . . .

Before I could think up any more arguments, I jerked awake. I looked down at Ol' Betsy's screen. There was no fancy lettering on it. Nothing at all. Just my superhero story with the cheesy ending.

I checked the room around me.

More of nothing. It was just like it was before I had nodded off. Just some seminormal kid struggling to do some seminormal homework.

Wait a minute! That was it!

Not it . . . but *him*! Willy Runeenoze! God hadn't wanted me doing fancy things, running off and having superhero adventures! He wanted me to help Willy! That's how I was supposed to help make the world a better place! By helping Willy right here and now . . . just like my story.

I couldn't believe it. God *did* show me. Over and over again. But I was so busy looking for the glory stuff that I kept ignoring the . . . *normal* stuff.

"How's this look?" Willy asked, holding up his math problem.

I glanced at his paper. To be honest, it looked pretty terrible. But that was okay, because I had all day to help him get it right. Granted, it wasn't much. I mean, I wouldn't be making the newspaper headlines or the TV shows. I wouldn't even be saving people from burning buildings (let alone paying for their dry cleaning) . . . at least for now.

Still, I would be making the world a better place.

Willy looked at me and sniffed. "Sir Mc, *ah-choo!* Doogle?"

I smiled and reached for the paper. "Just call me Wally," I said. "That sounds a lot more . . . normal. Now, let's see what we can do to fix this."

And so, together, we worked through the day . . . Willy-the-natural-born-sneezer and me, Wally-the-natural-born-loser. Then again, maybe I wasn't such a loser after all, not when I was

doing stuff like this. Don't get me wrong. I figured there would be plenty of time for adventures (and misadventures) in the future. But for
now I was perfectly content to be doing what was
in front of me here and now. Perfectly content to
be helping out where I could—in ways that were
perfectly and naturally . . . normal.

the incredible worlds of **Wally McDoogle**

You'll want to read them all.

IMAGER CHRONICLES

Another BILL MYERS series!

Who knew that the old rock found forgotten in the attic was actually the key to a fantastic alternative world? When Denise, Nathan, and Joshua stumble into the land of Fayrah, ruled by the Imager—the One who makes us in His image—they are drawn into wonderful adventures that teach them about life, faith, and the all-encompassing heart of God.

Book 1: THE PORTAL
(ISBN: 1-4003-0744-9)
Denise and Nathan meet a myriad of interesting characters in the wondrous world they've just discovered, but soon Nathan's selfish nature—coupled with some tricky moves by the evil Illusionist—gets him imprisoned. Denise and her new friends try desperately to free Nathan from the villain, but one of them must make an enormous sacrifice—or they will all be held captive!

Book 2: THE EXPERIMENT
(ISBN: 1-4003-0745-7)
Amateur scientist Josh unexpectedly finds himself whisked away to Fayrah with Denise. Quickly, he sees that not every-

thing can be explained rationally as he watches Denise struggle to grasp the enormity of the Imager's love. It's not until they meet the Weaver—who weaves the threads of God's plan into each life— that they both discover that understanding takes an element of faith.

Book 3: THE WHIRLWIND
(ISBN: 1-4003-0746-5)
The mysterious stone transports the three friends to Fayrah, where they find themselves caught between good and evil. There Josh falls under the spell of the trickster Illusionist and his henchman Bobok—who convince him that he can become perfect. Before they lose Josh in the Sea of Justice, Denise and Nathan must enlist the help of someone who is truly perfect. Will help come in time?

Book 4: THE TABLET
(ISBN: 1-4003-0747-3)
Denise finds a tablet with mysterious powers, and she is beguiled by the chance to fulfill her own desires—instead of trusting the Imager's plan. But when Josh and Nathan grasp the danger she faces, they work desperately to stop the Merchant of Emotions before he destroys Denise—and the whole world!

MEET WALLY McDOOGLE'S COUSIN

Trouble (and we're talking BIG trouble) runs in Wally's family. Follow his younger cousin Secret Agent Bernie Dingledorf and his trusty dog, Splat, as they try to save the world from the most amazing and hilarious events.

SECRET AGENT DINGLEDORF
... and his trusty dog, SPLAT
BY BILL MYERS